Book One in The JACK REACHER Cases

AUTHORDANAMES.COM

A MAN BUILT FOR JUSTICE

The Jack Reacher Cases #12

DAN AMES

Slogan Books, New York, NY

Praise for Dan Ames

"Fast-paced, engaging, original."

New York TIMES BESTSELLING
AUTHOR Thomas Perry

"Ames is a sensation among readers who
love fast-paced thrillers."

MYSTERY TRIBUNE

"Cuts like a knife."

Savannah Morning News

"Furiously paced. Great action."

New York TIMES BESTSELLING
AUTHOR Ben Lieberman

_____

The Jack Reacher Cases
_____

A MAN BUILT FOR JUSTICE

by

Dan Ames

Chapter 1

Belize

THE EASTERN COAST of Belize is a beauty to behold. One of the longest coral reefs in the world, it provides a natural seawall of sorts for the small country while also providing some of the best snorkeling on earth.

The water is clear and crystalline tinged with fragments of brilliant blue in all shades.

A Central American country, Belize's primary language is English, thanks to its history as a colony. This has helped the tiny nation become a mecca for expats from the US, Canada and parts of Europe.

A few miles from shore in water that sparkled with a stunning purity reserved for priceless diamonds, the young man swam with a natural grace. He was large for his age, with broad shoulders and long arms. His skin was tanned a deep brown. He was outfitted with flippers, a weight belt and a spear gun.

He was neither a tourist nor a native. He was simply known as a local to everyone but the true original populace.

None of that mattered to his quarry. The young man was seeking lionfish – an invasive species that had become the scourge of the Caribbean and beyond. The monstrous species had already done great damage to the coral reef and if not stopped, would most certainly destroy it completely.

The young man had made it a personal mission to destroy the lionfish. He speared dozens every day, bagged them and turned them over to the locals. Often, he would bag a lobster or grouper as well to have for lunch or dinner with his mother and grandmother.

He surfaced, took a deep breath and stocked his lungs with fresh oxygen, then dove. He swam past a coral outcropping and spotted his target species. The lionfish was a hideous-looking creature; the body of a fish with protective armor resembling that of a porcupine.

The young spear fisherman extended his spear gun, held his body steady and fired. The spear penetrated the lionfish in the center of its body. A perfect shot.

The hunter began retrieving his line when he sensed a shadow in his periphery.

A shark? he wondered.

He turned and saw a scuba diver less than twenty feet away. Odd, he thought. He hadn't seen another boat on the surface. So where had this diver come from? The young man noted that the scuba diver also had a spear gun. It was pointed directly at him.

The young man waved and pointed at the lionfish, as if to say, *I already got him.*

The scuba diver fired.

The young man's instinct was to move, to try to evade the shot, but there was no time. Simultaneously, the young man realized the other diver wasn't hunting lionfish.

As the spear pierced the boy's heart, he had registered who was the hunter and who was the hunted.

This knowledge came much too late.

Chapter 2

Lauren Pauling wrote the last of her checks.

Since the sale of her security firm, she had become a very wealthy woman. Yet, she had simple needs. Maybe if she'd made a fortune when she was in her twenties she would have flown to Monaco and blown it all on yachts, penthouses and parties. But at this point, she preferred to live a low-key kind of life.

Hence, the checks.

She insisted all of the donations she made be listed as anonymous and so far she'd helped support cancer research, children's hospitals, environmental organizations and finally, a national group dedicated to honoring members of the law enforcement community who'd died in the line of duty.

Pauling had served in the FBI and was proud

of the work she'd done. She'd worked with a lot of courageous, selfless individuals who had put their lives on the line for others. It made her feel good to still be helping alongside them, even if it wasn't in the field with a gun but rather in her co-op with a pen and a checkbook.

Satisfied with her choices, Pauling put away her financial paperwork, filed everything, and went into the kitchen. She had taken up intermittent fasting, which basically meant skipping breakfast and so far, it had been easy. But it left her pretty hungry at lunchtime.

Now, she scanned the contents of her fridge. She was about to pull out a plastic dish with some leftover quinoa and grilled chicken with asparagus when her doorbell rang.

She went to the video monitor by her door and saw an older man dressed in a light gray suit. He had on a hat and carried a cane and briefcase. Pauling pressed the intercom button.

"Yes?" she asked.

"Lauren Pauling?"

"Speaking."

"My name is Randall Naughton of the law firm Naughton, Mahoney and Peskar. I've come to speak with you about a very urgent matter."

"Am I being sued?" Pauling asked, half joking, half serious.

"No, this is about possibly retaining you for your services."

"I'm retired," Pauling said.

"I understand that, but my law firm has been tasked with helping in a highly delicate matter for which you may have some personal insight."

"What firm are you with again?"

"Naughton, Mahoney and Peskar."

Pauling had heard of the firm—a blue-chip group here in Manhattan catering to a fairly elite clientele.

"Okay, come on up," she said, and pressed the button that would allow the man entrance.

She shut the refrigerator door, went into her bedroom and clipped a holster with a small automatic to the back of her slacks, under her shirt.

Pauling was fairly sure the man was who he claimed to be, but she didn't believe in taking chances, either.

There was a soft knock on her door and Pauling opened it to reveal Naughton.

"Thank you for agreeing to see me," he said.

Up close, he was even older than she'd first thought. He was a small man with rounded shoulders and a face sporting red splotches. His suit was tailored, expensive and she spotted a Patek Philippe on his wrist.

"Come in," she said.

6

He entered and she caught the scent of coffee and subtle cologne.

"Would you like something to drink?" she asked.

"No thank you," he replied. "Is there a place—"

"Yes, right in here."

Pauling's co-op was a loft-style space with a living room area that faced tall windows overlooking Manhattan proper. A small dining nook, which she rarely used, was off the kitchen. That's where Naughton set his briefcase.

Pauling took the seat across from him. The table was made of dark wood, an African mahogany, and the chairs were matching, with brown leather cushions.

"What can I do for you, Mr. Naughton?"

He sighed as if he were about to deliver some extremely bad news.

"A young child is missing and may have been murdered in Belize."

Pauling waited. She didn't know anyone who lived in Belize. Her only relative was her sister, who lived in Portland and Pauling knew they were home in Oregon. Nowhere near Belize.

"That is not the official explanation," he continued.

"What is the official version?"

"Simply that he is missing. They suspect a

possible drowning but until they find the body, no one knows."

"I see."

She waited.

"The local authorities are searching for the body but in the meantime, we have been hired to investigate the matter. Obviously, our client feels there is more to the story."

"And how does this involve me?"

Another sigh, this time as if he were entering personal, sensitive territory. Pauling almost told him to just spit it out.

"The child was, or is, a young man who may have been the son of someone close to you."

Pauling's puzzled expression caused him to finish the thought.

"A man named Jack Reacher."

Chapter 3

His passport was British and he'd applied for it via an embassy in Stockholm. It was fake. He wasn't British, nor was he from Sweden.

However, when the authorities began their investigation of the missing young man in Belize, they would no doubt begin by looking at recent arrivals in the country.

It simply wouldn't do to have his real name appear on that list.

Now, he sat back in his seat on the plane and watched the waters of the Caribbean fall away below. His flight would take him to Rio de Janeiro where he would confirm the second half of the money had officially landed in his account.

Once that was established, he would partake in Rio's legendary nightlife for a few days before boarding a flight back to the US. He'd probably come into the country in New York and from there, take a rental car to Boston for his next assignment.

Unless, of course, he received instructions directing him elsewhere.

The plane reached cruising altitude and leveled off. The flight attendant began serving drinks in first class. He ordered himself a Bloody Mary.

This was going to be a very lucrative project, he thought to himself.

And the best part? It was only just beginning.

Chapter 4

"That's impossible," Pauling said.

Randall Naughton, the attorney who'd just dropped a bombshell on Pauling's dining room table held his hands up in defense.

"Maybe. Like I said, we need more information."

"What do you know about Jack Reacher?" Pauling asked.

"Me, personally?"

"Yes."

"Other than his connection to you, not one single thing."

"I see," Pauling said. "The idea Jack Reacher has a son is highly improbable. He does not live the kind of lifestyle suited for parenthood."

Naughton waited for her to continue.

"I also believe he is the kind of man who if he did bring a child into this world, he would most certainly be involved as a parent," Pauling continued. "He takes his responsibilities very seriously."

"As I said, more research is required, which is why I am here."

Pauling kept her frustration in check. She hadn't planned on something like this. The trip back to New York from Tallon's place had only occurred because of a conference she had wished to attend. The plan was for her to only be in the city for a few days before rejoining Tallon out west.

"What makes your client think this child is Reacher's?"

"I don't have an answer to that question."

"Why isn't your client satisfied with the local authorities? Won't they get to the bottom of this?"

"Again, I can't speak to my client's mindset. I'm only delivering a message."

With that, Naughton withdrew a file folder from his briefcase and slid it across the table.

"There is a check inside. It should be enough to cover at least a month of your work, plus travel and expenses."

"A month?" Pauling figured this would take a few days, tops. She glanced at the check. It was, in fact, triple what she would normally have charged if she were still running her business. The airline ticket also showed her destination: Belize.

"Have we reached an agreement?" Naughton asked.

After a moment, Pauling answered. "I'll let you know."

Chapter 5

Tallon's first thought on seeing the three men approach his casita was a disappointing one.

I'm going to have to move.

He had spent the better part of the day hunting in the canyons near his home on the border of Death Valley. The occasional mule deer could still be found in higher altitudes but he had no interest in them. Or any animal for that matter.

He did it mostly to stay in shape and to occasionally target shoot his rifle. It was a military-grade sniper rifle and he enjoyed its heft, the workout it provided hauling the heavy weapon up and down rough terrain was something he enjoyed. He'd done it many times in his life when he was hunting men.

Now, he had slowly descended from the ridge

behind his home. He'd moved here years ago and created a compound that delivered on all his needs; privacy, security and quiet.

After a long time as a soldier, mostly in Special Ops, and then as a private contractor working in some of the most dangerous areas in the world, Tallon had decided to slow down a bit. The casita was his favorite place in the world.

And now, a few locals had shown up.

They were old pals of his, in the sense that he'd beaten the hell out of two of them at a bar in town when they'd treated a female bartender rudely. Each fight had been a separate incident. The second time, the first one had brought rein-forcements.

Now, as he watched the idiots surround his small home, Tallon counted three of them.

If ever there was a case of subtraction by addition, this was it. The more of them there were, the dumber they got.

Tallon weighed his options. He could shoot all of them right now and call it a day. Bury the bodies in the desert.

He could have a little fun with them. Shoot one of them in the foot. Maybe one of the others in the arm. Tallon had spotted their 4x4 parked a few hundred yards from the house. He could put a few rounds into the engine block.

No, he didn't like any of those options.

Tallon preferred the direct approach.

He walked across the stretch of blood-red sand as the evening sun set. The three of them were trying to peek in his windows. Tallon could see one of them had a handgun stuck in the back of their jeans. The others were unarmed.

The sand made no sound as his feet took him across the stretch of ground and soon he was within ten feet of the trio. He brought his sniper rifle to his shoulder and put the crosshairs directly on center mass of the guy with the gun.

"Drop the gun," he said.

All three of them turned to look at him. Huey, Dewey and Screwy.

The guy with the gun looked at his buddies for advice. They didn't have any to offer so he dropped the gun on Tallon's porch.

"Kick it away," Tallon said.

The man complied.

"Okay, get off my porch and come over here."

They walked closer to him and Tallon raised the barrel of his rifle.

"I'm getting real tired of this," he said. "Why can't you just leave me in peace?"

The bigger of the two, the first one who'd gotten his ass beat back at the bar spoke for the others.

"You laid your hands on us. We ain't gonna let that go."

"You started it by slapping that bartender's ass, remember that?" Tallon countered. "I believe you even threw the first punch. You seem to have a highly selective memory."

"Don't make no difference," the grammarian said.

"Well, what do I have to do to make sure I never see you boys again?" Tallon said.

All three of them stood in silence.

"Well?"

The leader finally spoke. "Put down the gun and we'll finish this right now."

Tallon sighed, set the rifle on the ground next to him and walked closer to them.

"I just don't see the need for this."

He walked in as if he was going to start arguing with the leader but instead, he threw a right cross that whistled past the head of the guy in the middle and crashed into the jaw of the man who'd had the gun. Tallon had wanted to make sure he wouldn't make a run for the weapon.

It had happened so fast, and the guy in the middle was so shocked he was still standing when Tallon simply twisted and brought his arm back, elbow first. It smashed into the leader's temple and he crumpled like a wadded up dollar bill tossed into a collection basket.

That left the third man. He had raised his

hands and couldn't stop looking at his unconscious friends.

"Back the 4x4 up and take them away," Tallon said. He walked back and picked up his rifle.

He waited on the porch while the lone survivor loaded the inert slabs of beef into their vehicle and then drove off.

Once he was sure they were gone, he went in, set the alarm system and grabbed a beer from the fridge. His cell phone in hand, he took a long drink of cold beer and glanced at the screen.

A call was coming in.

From Pauling.

He slid his finger on the screen to accept the call and put the phone to his ear.

"Hi honey," he said.

Chapter 6

Tallon listened as Pauling described the proposal from Randall Naughton, attorney-at-law.

"So you're going to take the case?" he asked.

"I left him a message saying I would and I'd like you to come with me. Belize is beautiful, I've heard. Never been there, have you?"

"No," he said.

"Perfect, we can explore a new place together."

Tallon smiled at the thought.

"There is nothing I would rather do," he said. "Unfortunately, I leave for Mexico City in two days. It's an operation I committed to over two months ago and there's no way I can postpone it."

It hurt him to say it, because the idea of going to Belize with Pauling was the perfect opportunity for him to get away from the casita and put some distance between himself and his admirers here in town. He needed time to think if relocation was going to be required.

"Okay. How long do you think you'll be in Mexico City?" she asked him.

"Shouldn't take more than a week, at most. But you never know with these things. I could get there and it might be canceled altogether, or it could drag on for three weeks. As they say the situation is always…fluid."

"Why don't you fly down to Belize from there?" she asked. "You'll be pretty close. Should be a short flight."

"Will you still be there?"

"I'm not sure what I'm going to find, frankly," she said. "It all depends if the young man is found or not. If he's found, and he's alive, I won't have any reason to stick around longer than need be. If it goes the other way, then I'll probably be there for at least a week or two."

Tallon was tempted to tell her about his run-in with the locals who refused to let him be but he decided against it. One, he was slightly pissed off that he had already wasted the time it took him to kick their asses. Renting them headspace was not what he wanted, so he saw no reason to let them take up Pauling's time, too.

Besides, even though she wasn't the worrying kind, he didn't want to talk about an issue that didn't require her involvement. She had enough to think about with taking a new case and traveling.

They said their goodbyes and then Tallon realized he hadn't packed, either. He wasn't flying, though. They were going in to protect an American businessman who had fears he was being targeted by drug traffickers.

They were driving down to Mexico City.

Half of their load would be weapons.

Tallon hoped he wouldn't need to use them.

Chapter 7

Pauling hired a driver to take her to the airport. He put her bags in the trunk and she settled into the black sedan's back seat.

She sat back and went over her decision to investigate the young man's disappearance in Belize. She was supremely confident he was not Jack Reacher's illegitimate son. No way. Not Reacher's style at all. Oh, she knew he wandered all over the country and got into all kinds of scrapes. Hell, that's how she'd met him. And she also knew that he was the kind of guy who would attract lots of women. But an absentee father? No way. That went against everything Reacher stood for.

So why was she going?

It was a good question and not one she was sure held an answer. Curiosity, perhaps. Also, if she was being honest with herself, almost a sense of obligation. Jack Reacher was a good man. A friend. A former lover. What if the boy was actually his son? Did he even know? And what if it was true, but Reacher had no idea what was going on? Maybe he was walking around America with no idea that he'd fathered a son in Belize. Again, highly improbable but not totally impossible.

Pauling looked out the car's tinted windows. They were hitting traffic. The sound of honking horns and engines revving. A large semitrailer was crowding the lane next to them. She could practically see the individual granules of grit that coated the big vehicle's filthy side.

Her thoughts went back to the visit from the attorney, Naughton. Before she had called him and taken the case, she'd done some basic online research. The firm was certainly well-known, even in New York and although she saw no news reports of a missing boy in Belize, that wasn't unusual.

Countries who depended upon tourism as a primary source of revenue tended not to greet scandalous stories with an enthusiasm to share. News reports were often few and far between, swept under the rug for as long as possible. Someone said that all publicity is good publicity, but Pauling figured they hadn't had tourism in mind when they'd coined that phrase.

It didn't matter now, anyway, Pauling reflected. Her decision had been made.

She was about to get on a plane for Belize.

No point in second-guessing now.

Pauling arrived at the airport, went through security and for once, there were no delays.

She took her seat in first class and asked for a glass of white wine.

The flight seemed short and Pauling spent most of it thinking about the time she'd spent with Reacher. She felt a bit guilty about it, especially since her relationship with Michael Tallon had continued to grow.

Within a few short hours the turquoise waters of the Caribbean appeared below and Pauling couldn't help but feel a small jolt of excitement. She'd never been to the small central American country before, sitting just below the Yucatan Peninsula.

Pauling always felt a sense of adventure when she arrived at a destination that was entirely new to her. New experiences, sights and sensations were inherent in travel, and this trip was no exception.

It probably wouldn't be a thrill-a-minute and she certainly wished Tallon was with her.

The wheels touched down and Pauling once again marveled at the continuous surprises life had to offer. One minute she was going to attend a slightly boring conference in New York and fly back to Tallon's ranch, and less than 48 hours later she was touching down in Belize.

Whether this surprising development would be a good one or bad, she had no idea.

But it was time to find out.

Chapter 8

Once she was through Customs with her bags intact, Pauling made her way to the taxi stand and flagged down an ancient yellow car with four bald tires and an ancient driver.

As much as she would have liked to stay in Belize City, the small country's capital, it wasn't where she needed to be. Pauling knew the headquarters of the police department were here, but the scene of the disappearance was out on Ambergris Caye, the largest of Belize's islands, to the northeast of the city. It was the home of the second largest reef in the world and all of the visitors who flocked there.

Including, maybe but not likely, Jack Reacher's son.

Pauling had the taxi take her to the fastest of the sea ferries where she bought herself a one-way

Chapter 9

Pauling sidled up next to a man, an obvious tourist, with sunburned skin and a floppy straw hat.

"What's going on?" she asked.

"Drunk couple from Canada," the man responded. "The husband passed out and the wife panicked. Happens all the time. Those Canadians act like they're big boozers but down here, they're amateurs."

He turned and walked back toward a dockside bar. There were tables right up against the wooden railing and everyone was watching the scene on the beach. And drinking.

Pauling studied the police vehicle. It was a white Land Rover, at least a dozen years old. The cop, a woman, wore a tan short-sleeved shirt, a blue skirt, hose and black flats. Her brown skin was smooth and flawless, her black hair pulled back into a tight bun. Unlike most of the tourists, she wasn't sweating. Not a single drop.

"Does this happen a lot?" Pauling asked as she approached the policewoman.

"Once in a while, ma'am, but everything's going to be okay."

The woman's English was excellent – it was the country's main language, but accented. Pauling's research had told her the locals often spoke a mix of Spanish and Belizean Creole that someone had coined "kitchen Spanish."

"Any news on that missing boy?" Pauling asked.

The woman turned and seemed to really see her for the first time. The policewoman's eyes looked over Pauling's shoulder as if to see if anyone else was listening.

"Not that I know of, no."

"Are you handling the investigation?"

"No."

"Who is?"

"That would be Deputy Jalisco."

She gestured to a man in a golf cart on the other side of the ambulance. He had on a black cap with a badge on its peak, tan shirt and pants, and black shoes. His shirt had epaulets and a black rope went down his left shoulder.

Pauling walked over to him.

"Deputy Jalisco?"

Up close, she realized he was a big man. Way over six feet, for sure, even though he was sitting down. And massive. Broad shoulders, a big belly and a round face. The golf cart actually leaned slightly to the left because of his bulk.

He peered at her from under the visor of his cap. He didn't smile or answer.

"I was just asking your officer about the boy that went missing while spearfishing. Any word on what happened?"

"Who are you?" he asked.

"My name's Lauren."

He ignored her. Didn't answer. Didn't even look back at her.

"Deputy? Did you hear my question?"

"Are you a member of the family?" he asked.

"No, but–"

"Then I have nothing to say to you." He punched the gas pedal on the golf cart and it sped past her, kicking up a cloud of dust in its wake.

Pauling watched him go. The ambulance followed as did the officer in the Land Rover. When they all turned the corner, she glanced up at the people watching from the bar. They were no longer interested in the beach.

She walked to the bar and glanced off to her right. A swimming area had been cordoned off with a swim-up bar. A pale man with a big fish-white belly was floating in an inflatable armchair. In his hand was a huge drink. He gave her a drunken, lopsided grin.

"Holy shit," he said. "Hello, hot stuff. Why don't you strip down and join me in the water for a drink?"

Pauling laughed in spite of herself.

"Tempting, but I'll take a rain check," she said, and walked into the bar.

Chapter 10

Dozens of fish mounted on the walls told Pauling the local taxidermist was probably a very busy guy. A wood floor, dusty with bits of straw here and there, also told her the drinking establishment was as low-key as Ambergris Caye itself.

Rock music played in the background. *Van Halen*, Pauling thought.

She walked up to the bar and was met by a woman with skin as dark and dried out as shoe leather. She had white hair and blue eyes.

"What'll you have?" the woman asked her.

"How about a bottle of beer. Have anything local?"

"Sure do," the woman answered. She reached down, brought up a dark brown bottle with a white and blue label and the word *Belikin* across the front.

"Brewed right here in Belize," the woman said.

"Thanks, what's your name?" Pauling asked.

"Cass."

The woman held out a wrinkled hand.

"Lauren," Pauling said. They shook hands.

"What brings you down to our little slice of paradise?" Cass asked.

"A friend of mine recommended I visit. A big guy named Jack Reacher, you remember him coming here?"

Cass tilted her head to one side. "No, but you can imagine the number of folks who've passed by here."

"Jack is a huge guy – 6'5" with massive shoulders. He has a presence, you might say."

Cass shook her head. "Doesn't ring a bell. Are you here alone?"

Pauling nodded. "Yeah, I just sold my company in New York and wanted to treat myself to a vacation."

"Well, this is the place to do it." Cass glanced around and then leaned in closer to Pauling. "You should be careful, though. A woman alone down here is safe, but it still pays to keep your eyes open, know what I mean?"

"I do. I heard about that boy who disappeared. What's the story with that?"

34

"Sad, sad," Cass replied. "Rubi is beside herself."

"Rubi?"

"Rubi Gemmot. The boy's mom. She owns Rubi's Coffee and I see her every morning. She's handling it well because she's tough. But still, it can't be easy."

Reacher. Coffee. Pauling thought the odds may have shifted with new possibilities.

They talked a bit longer and Pauling enjoyed her beer. It was heavy, almost like a German brew and it was strong. She finished her beer, thanked Cass and walked back out onto the street.

The sun was blasting down and golf carts passed her by. Pauling decided to walk. She keyed in Rubi's Coffee on her phone and saw that it was along the northwest side of San Pedro, about a mile and a half from where she now stood.

A walk would do her good.

She set off at a brisk pace, moving around the tourists and locals in no hurry to get anywhere. The golf carts seemed to outnumber cars by at least three to one. The street was surprisingly busy, but everyone moved at an island pace.

Pauling passed dozens of shops and cafes and several tiny markets offering booze and ice cream.

She spotted Rubi's Coffee – a white building with orange trim and green shutters. It looked like there was perhaps an upstairs living space and the coffee shop was on the ground floor. The building was neat, clean and appeared well taken care of. Pauling went to the door but it was locked. She knocked on the door and waited.

No one seemed to be around.

That's odd, she thought.

She dialed the phone number for Rubi's Coffee but there was no answer. Pauling checked her watch. Maybe it was siesta time. Or maybe the shop was only open in the mornings.

She decided to check back first thing in the morning.

Pauling retraced her steps and when she figured she was about halfway back to her condo, she was sure of one thing.

Someone was following her.

Chapter 11

The man with the British passport sat on his rooftop patio overlooking the sprawl of Rio de Janeiro below.

It had been a wonderful three days.

His payment for the job in Belize had come through like clockwork. He'd siphoned off a little less than a hundred thousand and sent the rest to his numbered account in Switzerland. From there, some of it would be routed to an account in the Cayman Islands. He preferred to keep money in both locations, just in case one was compromised.

Flush with cash, he had thoroughly enjoyed all of the carnal options available in Rio. He was reminded of that expression: *I spent my money on booze, drugs and women. The rest, I wasted.* It made him smile, partly because it was true. He'd stocked his penthouse suite in the swankiest hotel in town with the best tequila money could buy, a huge bag of cocaine, and an endless stream of the most beautiful and willing prostitutes in the world.

Now, it was morning and the only thing he was enjoying was a cup of rich, black coffee. Behind him, in the room, the last two prostitutes had left. One female and one transsexual. Once the booze and drugs took hold, he preferred things to get as wicked and sordid as possible. Last night was the ultimate in frenzied hedonism.

He checked his watch, a Richard Mille worth about a hundred thousand dollars.

It would be bittersweet to leave Rio, but his next job was just as lucrative as the one in Belize, mostly because it was for the same employer and really constituted just a continuation of the work he'd done previously.

Simply in a different location.

But it would be a similar target.

The man went back into the room and began to pack. He noted with amusement the prostitutes had made off with the rest of the unused cocaine. That was fine. He'd intended them to take it.

When he returned one day, maybe he'd run into them again.

And make them pay.

Chapter 12

Pauling had first spotted the man in the reflection of a store window. He stood out because of a white short-sleeved shirt with some sort of metal clip or button on the left breast pocket that caught the reflection of the sun. She'd seen him on the way down to the coffee shop and now, she had just seen him again. What were the odds that he had planned to walk both down the strip and back, just as she had?

Not likely.

Pauling went around the block, picked up her pace and reappeared south of where she'd started.

She looked for the man but didn't see him.

It was always a possibility that her imagination had created the threat. Maybe it wasn't the same guy, or maybe he'd had a legitimate reason to follow her path.

Pauling wasn't going to worry about it. By the time she made it back to her condo, dusk was setting in and she was tired. The flight, the shock of being back in a tropical climate had left her slightly out of her normal timeline.

She wasn't hungry and decided to go to bed early and start fresh in the morning. The night was quiet and peaceful. In the morning, she was awakened by the sound of waves hitting the shore and in the distance, a motorcycle racing down one of the streets.

Pauling showered, dressed, and went down to the building's lobby where she'd been told coffee was available in the morning. There was a silver pot plugged into the wall by a door marked *Office*. The door was open and two people were chatting. One was a man dressed in a freshly ironed yellow shirt, tan shorts and fisherman's sandals.

The woman he was speaking with was petite, with long black hair, an oval face and a button nose. She turned and looked at Pauling.

That's a beautiful woman, Pauling thought.

Then she noted the paper bag in the woman's hand. It read *Rubi's Coffee*.

The man was saying something about a tropical storm on the way.

Pauling poured herself a cup and when the office door closed and the woman turned to leave, Pauling said, "Good morning."

The woman glanced her way. "Hello," she said. Pauling could see the dark circles under her eyes, the worry lines across her forehead.

"Is this your coffee?" Pauling asked, lifting the cup. "It's delicious."

"Yes."

"So you're Rubi?"

"I am."

The woman glanced at the door and then back at Pauling.

"Are you walking back to your shop?" Pauling asked.

"Yes."

"Do you mind if I walk with you?"

"Of course not."

They left and Pauling said, "My name's Lauren. I just arrived yesterday for some vacation and I'd heard you had the best coffee on the island."

"Thank you, but I'm the only one who sells my own coffee on the island."

"It's very good," Pauling said.

They walked down the street. It was morning and there were very few people out and about.

"I'm sorry to bring this up but I heard your son is missing, is there any news?"

Rubi's face lost its color and she bowed her head as if she'd been struck.

"No."

"If there's anything I can do to help, I used to work in law enforcement back in the US."

Rubi stopped. "Why do you want to help me?" she asked. "Do I know you? Have we met?"

"No, but a friend of mine thought I could help. His name is Jack Reacher."

Rubi's face was blank. *Either she had never heard the name, or she's a very good poker player*, Pauling thought.

"How can you help me?" Rubi asked. "The police said they are doing what they can."

They had resumed walking. "To be honest, I'm not sure," Pauling answered. "Perhaps with your approval I could speak with Deputy Jalisco. Maybe see what they've uncovered so far and what their plan is for the investigation."

Rubi abruptly stopped again. "No. That would be a bad idea."

"Why?"

"Look, I'm not sure who you are or why you're here, but Peter will be found, I am confident of that," Rubi said. "God will watch over us and everything will be okay. I'm sure of that."

Pauling heard the doubt in the woman's voice, despite her words.

"Do you have a photo of Peter?" Pauling asked.

The woman sighed. Pauling felt guilty asking, knowing that seeing a photo of her son would probably bring the woman more anguish but she had to see the young man.

Rubi slid a cell phone from a pocket in her skirt, swiped the screen until she had an image. She turned the phone toward Pauling.

The young man was handsome. He had dark skin, dark hair.

And blue eyes.

Chapter 13

There was no shortage of options for spearfishing excursions on Ambergris Caye. In fact, there were probably more boats than people in San Pedro.

Pauling decided to rent a scooter so she could cover more ground faster. Not that San Pedro was big, but it would save her time walking back and forth. She used her corporate credit card to rent a fairly new Honda Ruckus. It was made of a metal frame with a single seat and knobby off-road-type tires. There was no shifting of gears and the brakes were good.

Pauling drove it to the dock from which the young Peter Gemmot had supposedly departed for his spearfishing excursion. However, she had no idea of the name of the boat or its captain, if it even had one. It was always possible that Peter had his own boat. A 14-foot aluminum fishing boat with an old outboard wouldn't cost much around here. Pauling had considered asking Rubi about it, but the woman clearly hadn't wanted her nosing around, so she'd decided against asking.

She parked the Ruckus and used the lock that had come with it to secure the scooter to a telephone pole.

Pauling walked onto the dock. The smell of the ocean was pungent. A mixture of fish, rotting seaweed and gasoline. There were at least a dozen boats in the process of coming or going. Most of them were manned by locals. Probably fishermen who supplied the town's restaurants with fresh seafood and shellfish.

A few bigger boats carrying a load of tourists sporting snorkeling gear also set out for the reef in the distance.

An older man with a kind face was repairing a large casting net. Pauling approached him.

"Hello," she said.

"Hiya," he answered in accented English.

"I'm trying to help Rubi find her son, Peter. Do you know if he used his own boat for spearfishing?"

Pauling had opted for the direct approach. She figured it was a small town and everyone probably knew about the boy's disappearance.

"Yes," the old man said.

"Yes he had his own boat?"

The old man nodded.

"Did he keep it here?"

The man put down the cast net and walked out toward the end of the dock. Pauling followed.

When he reached a narrow slip between two charter fishing boats, he pointed at the water.

The old man shrugged his shoulders as if he had no reason why the boy hadn't returned.

He left her to return to his net repair and Pauling studied the empty slip. There was nothing but a coil of old stained rope. The water was clear, with some soggy weeds pushed up against the dock's piling.

The boats on either side were large, with racks of fishing rods pointing toward the sky. There was no sound or movement on either one.

"You are going to get yourself into trouble," a voice said behind her.

Pauling turned and saw the female San Pedro police officer she'd seen before. The woman had on the same tan shirt, blue skirt and black flats. Her hair was pulled back into a tight bun. This time, however, she had on a pair of Ray-Ban sunglasses with gold frames. The lenses were coffee-colored and Pauling could just make out the woman's eyes.

"How so?" Pauling asked. "What's your name, by the way?"

"I am Officer Novelo and if you continue to

ask questions about the missing boy you will upset Deputy Jalisco. One of his men noticed you walking down to Rubi's Coffee yesterday. He reported back to Deputy Jalisco. You don't want to make him angry."

Pauling had been right; San Pedro was a very small town. Word traveled fast.

"Did he send you here to tell me that?"

"I simply offered it as a bit of friendly advice. We try to take care of our visitors here as best we can."

Pauling sensed the implied threat.

"So how is the investigation going?" she asked anyway. "Were there any witnesses? Any evidence of foul play?"

"Have a good day, Ms. Pauling," Officer Novelo said.

She turned and walked away. On her hip, a walkie talkie came to life.

Pauling followed the cop and overheard the message.

All units to Sapphire Beach.

Novelo stopped and looked back at Pauling. Her expression was blank but Pauling knew exactly what was happening.

They'd found something…or someone.

Chapter 14

Pauling waited for Novelo to leave in her police golf cart and then she went to her scooter, unlocked it, fired it up and followed. She had remembered seeing the Sapphire Beach Resort on the northeast end of Ambergris Caye.

It made sense to Pauling; ocean currents most likely would have taken a dead body in that direction, although she was no expert. It was also a fairly wild guess as she had no idea when or where the body may or may not have gone into the water.

Nevertheless, she had a feeling urgent requests for police matters weren't all that common and combined with the way Novelo had looked at her after receiving the call, Pauling had a fairly good idea what was happening.

It was nearly ten miles from the heart of San

Pedro to Sapphire Beach. There was virtually no traffic, only a few tourists in golf carts either coming or going from the resort area. Pauling loved the feel of the scooter – the air was invigorating and the little engine was more than enough to get her there.

She passed very few signs of development, save for the various structures along the beach. On the other side of the road was mostly thick stands of palms and mangroves.

Eventually, she saw the flashing lights of one of San Pedro's police cars. It was the Land Rover. Two police golf carts were next to the Rover.

Pauling cruised past, spotted a waterfront juice bar with a bike rack. She pulled in, locked the Ruckus to the rack, and to appear as if she were there for some other reason, ordered a juice. Pauling didn't want anything to drink but felt she couldn't use the rack for free, plus, it gave her something to do as she wandered up toward the scene at the beach.

There were at least a dozen people down along the surf. They had formed a rough semi-circle and Pauling could see the immense bulk of Deputy Jalisco at the center.

She walked closer, circling the group until she could spot the object of attention.

It was a body, although it had spent some time in the water and had possibly been the target for hungry sharks. Pauling could only catch tiny glimpses and wasn't exactly sure what she was seeing.

A 4x4 Chevy SUV with a decal on the side designating it as an ambulance backed onto the beach. Two men wearing blue and white shirts exited the vehicle with a stretcher and met Jalisco.

Pauling edged her way closer to the group. She still didn't have a good look at the body.

"What's happening?" she asked a woman to her right. The woman was pale with freckles, and answered with a British accent.

"That boy who went missing, we think," the woman whispered.

Pauling watched as the human remains were loaded onto the stretcher. There was no way to tell if it was male or female. The remains didn't even look human.

She wondered if San Pedro even had a coroner or a crime scene officer. Not that there would be any evidence left, at this point. The only real clues would be on the body itself. Plus, the crowd had probably destroyed any other evidence that may have washed ashore.

The crowd made way for the stretcher and as Jalisco walked by, he spotted Pauling.

His face darkened at the sight of her but he didn't say anything.

The Chevy was loaded and soon pulled back

onto the road, heading toward San Pedro. Jalisco and Novelo got into the Land Rover and followed.

Pauling tossed her drink into the trash, went back to her Ruckus, unlocked it, and followed the procession back into town.

She felt a deep sadness as she thought of the cops breaking the news to Rubi. During her career in law enforcement, she'd had to inform loved ones that their family member had perished. It was a difficult job and one that had to be handled just right.

Pauling wondered if Jalisco would break the news gently.

In the meantime, she would go back to her condo and break the news to Randall Naughton.

Something told her the attorney wasn't going to be surprised.

Chapter 15

Judging by the severity of the glare she'd received from Deputy Jalisco, Pauling figured her time might better be served by going back to her condo and laying low for a few hours.

She keyed in the code to the gate and drove inside the compound. Pauling locked up the scooter and went into her condo. The sliding glass doors faced the ocean and Pauling opened them, sat in one of the outdoor wicker chairs and dialed the phone number for Randall Naughton on her cell phone.

Surprisingly, he answered himself. Pauling was expecting an assistant to answer.

"Naughton? It's Lauren Pauling, in Belize."

"Yes."

"I believe the body of Peter Gemmot has been

found. I'll need to confirm, of course, as best as I can, but I'm fairly certain it's him."

"I understand. I'll wait to pass along the news to my client."

"One more thing," Pauling said, interrupting him as it sounded like he was about to hang up. "I spoke with the boy's mother, Rubi. And as I mentioned before, I'm fairly certain the boy is not Jack Reacher's son. I questioned her, even brought up Reacher's name and described him, she had never met him. Showed no sign of recognition."

"Very well," Naughton replied. "Still, you must confirm the boy's identity before I'm comfortable with you wrapping things up down there. More importantly, I want you to be able to find out if the authorities think this was an accident or something else."

"Yes, that's my goal," Pauling said. "The local police are not big on sharing but I may have found a way around them."

She hoped she'd made a positive impression on Rubi and she could get the necessary information, eventually, from the mother. Pauling wanted to be sensitive, though, and not rush in and start asking questions, less than twenty-four hours after the woman learns her son is dead.

If that turned out to be the case.

She was confident it would be.

Pauling disconnected the call and sat on the

balcony, watching the gentle waves roll into shore. Because of the reef, this stretch of beach didn't receive the big waves surfers love.

She thought of calling Tallon but decided against it. Instead, she went back into the room, grabbed a bottle of beer and sat back in the chair and gazed out at the ocean.

I could get used to this, she thought.

Chapter 16

He took all of the usual precautions.

From Rio he flew to Mexico City using the same identity. However, once in Mexico, he picked up a second set of papers that now showed he was a Frenchman traveling on business and promptly booked a flight to New York. Once in New York, he rented a car under yet another identity and drove to Boston.

There, he went to a prearranged location; a shopping mall on the outskirts of the city. He drove to a commercial mail drop and used a key he'd been given to open a medium-sized shipping box. In it were more identification papers, as well as a gun, ammunition and sound suppressor.

Back on the freeway, he zipped right through the center of Boston, taking advantage of the time period between rush hours and soon found himself breaking free of the highway and turning onto Cape Cod.

He used Highway 6, the mid-Cape freeway and then changed his mind and went south to Highway 28, past Hyannis Port and the playground of the Kennedy family.

Eventually, he stopped at a motel that included *by the sea* in its name, which made him laugh. He parked, went inside, and booked a room, paying cash in advance.

He left his suitcase closed, but opened the package containing the handgun. He looked it over carefully to make sure it wasn't the recipient of any sabotage efforts. The man had known others in his profession who'd been betrayed by their employers. Those betrayals had taken the form of malfunctioning weapons that left them either dead, compromised, or arrested.

He had no intention of letting that happen.

The man looked at his watch.

He would rest for a few hours. His target was occupied at the moment but soon, the window of opportunity would open.

The man stretched out on the bed, glanced out his window.

He saw the parking lot.

And wondered what part of *by the sea* they were talking about.

Chapter 17

Pauling waited until mid-morning to make her move. She'd gotten a coffee at a local café figuring Rubi would have other things on her mind than opening her shop and going forward with business as usual.

There was no one else in the café and Pauling idly scrolled through news on her phone. There was a text from Tallon that he'd landed in Mexico City and begun his security project.

A few emails from old colleagues talking about new or strange cases they'd been assigned. These were folks still working for the FBI or as investigators for her old firm. The one she'd sold.

A day didn't go by where she wondered if she'd done the right thing selling her firm. And she always wound up in the same place; knowing she had, in fact, done what was best. The time had been right and so had the price. She'd taken the firm as far as she'd wanted to and been more than amply rewarded.

Pauling always recognized these thoughts for what they were: separation anxiety, nothing more.

She finished her coffee and strolled down the street toward Rubi's shop. As it came into view, Pauling spotted the white Land Rover favored by the San Pedro police.

Deputy Jalisco was standing on the front porch and before Pauling could react, the man was waving her forward.

"Shit," Pauling muttered under her breath. She hadn't wanted to have any contact with the man but there had been nowhere to go. Pauling couldn't have ducked or pretended she hadn't seen him.

Instead, she walked directly up to Jalisco.

"Good morning," she said.

"Why is it I see you everywhere I go?" he asked.

"You're lucky?" Pauling responded with a smile.

The big man ignored her and walked down the steps. They creaked under his weight. Jalisco walked right up to her, getting in her personal space. Pauling could smell him; a mix of body sweat, cigar smoke and coffee.

"I believe I asked you to how do you say it — to mind the business that is yours, not mine."

"You never actually said that," Pauling pointed out. "Besides, I was just coming by to buy some coffee. You know, Rubi is the only one on the island who grows her own coffee."

Jalisco's face showed no traces of humor.

"Rubi's son is dead," he said. "He drowned. It was an accident. That all is you need to know."

"That was fast."

"Yes, he probably died quickly and painlessly."

"No, not the death. I mean establishing the cause of death. Has an autopsy been performed already? I mean, wow, even the best police departments take at least a day or two to determine cause of death. You guys are incredibly fast. What's your secret?"

Jalisco's dark eyes clouded over. For a moment, Pauling wondered if she'd let the sarcasm go too far and tensed. Jalisco looked like he wanted to take a swing at her.

"If I have to talk to you again, it will be to tell you that you are under arrest for interfering in an investigation," he said as he turned to walk to the Land Rover.

"What investigation? You said he drowned. Isn't the investigation over?"

Jalisco ignored her, fired up the Land Rover and sped off in a cloud of dust.

Pauling watched him go and then took out her phone.

Chapter 18

The woman in the penthouse apartment with views of Central Park stood with her arms folded in front of her.

The phrase reverberated in her mind; *the boy is dead.*

Although she played no small part in the scene down in Belize, she felt no great sense of pride or satisfaction.

It was no different than looking at one's bank account to ascertain that a certain deposit had been made.

The woman turned and walked back toward the fireplace in the living room. She'd ordered a small fire built to take the edge off the chill in the air.

In her mind, the sequence of events she had longed to pull off unfurled before her, a golden road with no bumps or detours, just the feeling of gathering speed and wind in the hair.

The news was good.

Rayce had done his job, and done it well. Something that should have gone without saying considering how much she was paying him.

But what it marked was even better.

Progress.

Chapter 19

"I see," Naughton responded.

Pauling had returned to her condo and was now on the phone with the attorney. She had just told him the news: Peter Gemmot was dead and the authorities were saying it was an accident, that he had drowned.

"I've also been warned by the head of the San Pedro Police that if I continue to ask questions, I may very well find myself under arrest."

There was a pause and Pauling thought she heard the sound of someone typing on a computer keyboard.

"Hello?" she asked.

"Yes," Naughton answered. "No need for that. You've done what was asked, the boy has been found and the cause of death determined. We'll consider the case closed and I'll let my client know. Please send us your final bill and we will pay it upon receipt."

Pauling was about to ask another question but her phone beeped and she realized that Naughton had already disconnected.

That was strange, she thought.

She was about to redial when there was a knock at her door.

Pauling crossed the room and opened the door, half expecting to see Jalisco and a couple of his cronies ready to place her under arrest.

To her surprise, it was Rubi.

"Come in," Pauling said.

The woman entered.

"I'm so sorry to have heard the news about your son," Pauling said. "Can I get you something? Water? Coffee?"

"No." And then, "thank you."

Rubi looked around the condo and her eyes settled on a chair next to the door. She sat in it quickly, as if she might fall.

Pauling took the edge of the loveseat across from her. Pauling wasn't surprised by Rubi's disheveled appearance. The woman clearly hadn't slept and although she didn't appear to be in a case of full-fledged shock, clearly confirmation of the death of her son, which she had probably deep down suspected, had left her fragile.

Pauling decided to wait for the woman to speak.

After a few moments, Rubi took a deep breath. "They say he drowned."

"Yes," Pauling replied.

"I don't believe them." Rubi lifted her head and looked directly at Pauling. "He was like a shark in the water. The boy detested alcohol and drugs. It was morning. The weather was calm. Impossible. Just…impossible."

Pauling considered her response carefully. "Did the police tell you why they think he drowned?"

"No. Of course not."

It occurred to Pauling she had no idea why the woman was here.

"What are you going to do?" she asked.

"What do you know about all of this?" Rubi said. "Why are you here?"

"Like I said, I was asked by a friend, Jack Reacher, to see if I could help find the boy?"

"Who is this Jack Reacher? You asked me before about him."

Pauling wanted to be careful. Technically, she was lying. Obviously, Reacher hadn't hired her or asked her to look into this, it was just her way of seeing if Rubi had been involved with him. So far, it appeared she hadn't. But Pauling also didn't know how to explain the truth. Instead, she asked, "What about your son's father?"

"What about him?" Rubi said. Her face had flinched and now Pauling saw anger in the woman's eyes.

"Where–"

"He's dead. He died ten years ago in a car accident in the city. Why?"

"If you think your son's death might not have been an accident–"

"It had nothing to do with my dead husband," Rubi snapped. "That was long ago. No, this is something else. I thought you might know something. I think I was wrong to come here."

She got to her feet.

"Wait–" Pauling said, but Rubi opened the door to the condo and left, shutting it firmly behind her.

The sound of the woman's footsteps retreated in the distance and Pauling glanced out the window at the ocean beyond. It was calm. The water shone like a diamond surrounded by sapphires. Rubi's words made sense to her. How did a fit young man manage to drown in calm water?

Pauling supposed there could be a number of answers, but they would most likely remain a mystery without an objective autopsy and full-on investigation. Something that didn't appear to be likely in San Pedro. Not if Jalisco had anything to do with it.

She retrieved her suitcase and began packing for her trip back to New York. The case may have been closed, but Pauling wasn't satisfied.

She wasn't sure this was going to be the end of it, at least, not for her, anyway.

Chapter 20

Rayce opened his eyes. Instantly, he remembered where he was. A cheap motel *by the sea.*

He had dozed only briefly, enough to sharpen his senses and make him feel rested.

He sat up in bed, let his mind fully come awake, then crossed the room to the desk where he'd set the pistol with its suppressor. He contemplated leaving it there but instead, tucked it behind his belt at the small of his back and threw on a light jacket. He went to the lobby of the motel where he'd spotted a coffeemaker. He filled a white Styrofoam cup and drank the cheap brew in several gulps. When he'd checked in he'd already confirmed there were no security cameras in place.

Back in his room, he wiped away any trace evidence of his stay and went out to his car. There was a good possibility he would come back if his first trip proved unsuccessful. Still, it was better to have everything on one's person, to be as mobile as possible.

Rayce drove the rental car out along Highway 28 East. He had always envisioned Cape Cod as an arm the state of Massachusetts was holding out and bending as if to show off their bicep muscle. His destination was the crook of the elbow, before the rest of the arm pointed north.

It was quaint Americana, Rayce observed. Everything made to look antique colonial, as if the residents had just finished overthrowing the evil British empire.

He turned at a junction that featured a large convenience store on one side and yet another motel on the other. Soon, he was winding his way into a suburban area.

Rayce was looking for a school and soon found it. He pulled up at an intersection two blocks away and watched as parents in minivans arrived, parked as close as they could and waited for the bell to ring.

From his pocket he pulled a sheet of paper that contained an image of the child he was looking for and the vehicle. Every day, at the same time, the child left the school, walked to the same spot and got into the same vehicle.

Rayce was looking for a minivan whose license

plate matched the numbers on the sheet of paper. He shut off the engine of his rental car, pocketed the keys and walked. A block and a half north of where he had parked he spotted the vehicle and its matching plate.

Walking past, he pulled out his cell phone as if he had just received a call and then turned at the next block. He circled back and heard the school bell ring. Rayce walked slowly back toward the target vehicle and stopped just beyond the last parked car. He wore black dress slacks, a collared shirt and a dark blue jacket. With his dark hair, and good looks, Rayce looked like a caring father meeting his child after school.

Soon, the children appeared and as they made their way to the parents-in-waiting, Rayce spotted the boy. He was tall, with broad shoulders and he carried his head high. A sign of confidence. Most tall kids have poor posture, self-conscious of their height.

Someone had taught the boy well, Rayce thought. Which was a shame.

He pushed off from his spot across the street and came up behind the minivan. The gun was now in his hand, down by his side.

As he came around, the boy had taken off his backpack and was holding it in front of him, digging around toward the bottom, looking for something.

Rayce raised his gun and fired two shots into the center of the boy's chest.

The boy flew backward and landed on the sidewalk.

"Hey!" A woman in a car was pointing toward Rayce. He took a step forward just as a police car came into view.

Rayce ducked into the yard of the house to his left, raced across the backyard, jumped a fence, and came out on the street where he'd parked his rental car.

He had no idea if the cop had seen him, or was just cruising by. But the woman who'd shouted at him was no doubt flagging the cops down.

Behind him, as if to verify his train of thought, he heard a siren, and then the sound of cars honking.

Rayce jumped into the rental car, put it in gear and drove away, quickly, but not enough to draw attention.

He wouldn't be going back to the motel.

There wasn't even satisfaction at having completed his job.

Only four words were stuck in his head.

On to the next.

Chapter 21

After considering some different flight options, Pauling had decided to go back to New York. For one thing, Tallon was in Mexico and was working so it wasn't like she could join him. Her only living relative was her sister, who lived in Portland. Pauling had just been out to see them.

Especially considering how quickly she'd left New York, it made sense to go back, wait for Tallon to finish his gig in Mexico City, and then go from there.

She took the ferry back to the mainland, caught a flight and was soon unlocking the door to her loft. It felt good to be back home. She unpacked, showered and changed.

There weren't any messages and she knew in the morning she would have to go out and get some food. The only thing in the fridge was a bottle of chardonnay which she uncorked. After pouring herself a glass, she checked her email, expecting a reply from Randall Naughton.

But there wasn't one.

She had emailed him her final bill during the flight back to the States. It was the kind of thing that usually deserved a response of sorts. Pauling had a funny feeling about the situation–it had begun when Naughton had so abruptly ended their conversation and her investigation. It had also been odd the way she'd asked him a question and it seemed like there had been a pause while he was typing. The whole thing had been a little strange to begin with.

Obviously, she'd gone because of the possibility the missing child was Reacher's. That was something she was now convinced simply wasn't true. Women tended not to forget Jack Reacher and she was positive Rubi wasn't lying.

So why had Naughton's client suspected otherwise? More importantly, *who* was Naughton's client?

Pauling knew she could just let the whole thing go, but she didn't want to.

She decided then and there that she wasn't going to let it slide. Pauling found her iPad and looked up Naughton's firm. She was going to pay them a visit in person. Pauling found the firm's website and jotted down the address. While she was there, she clicked on the section of the website marked *About Us*. The principals, including Naughton, were listed but there were no photographs.

She found a link to their public relations section and clicked her way through various news releases until she found one that included a group shot of the head of the firm.

Pictured in the center was Randall Naughton.

Pauling put down her wineglass and stared at the picture.

Because the man in the photo in no way resembled the Randall Naughton who'd sent her to Belize.

Chapter 22

At one point during a relatively recent case, Pauling's home had been broken into. After that discovery, she'd installed the most technologically advanced security system money could buy.

Importantly, everything was recorded and stored on a server in the cloud. Which made it very convenient for her to rewind the footage back to that moment when the man posing as Randall Naughton had come to her door.

She was able to perform an image capture of the man's face, download it to her computer and sharpen the focus via some very basic editing software. Pauling then sent the image to a clandestine service run by a former client. It had access to various government databases including the department of motor vehicles of New York.

It was a major disappointment, she thought.

She was mostly frustrated with herself. Why had she not done a better job of confirming the man who'd hired her? It angered her as well. Maybe she'd been out of the game too long. Deep down, she knew that wasn't true. Even though she'd sold her firm, she and Tallon had kept busy…and then some.

One thing she knew for sure: she was going to get to the bottom of this case, one way or another.

She finished unpacking, went to bed and in the morning, the first thing she did was check her email to see if her former client had identified the man.

He had.

The man's name was certainly not Randall Naughton.

It was Evan Austin.

There was some basic biographical information, but it was one of the last things listed that caught Pauling's eye:

Occupation: actor.

Chapter 23

Pauling took the elevator down to the underground parking structure. She climbed into her Mercedes SUV and followed her navigation to the Brooklyn Heights neighborhood, home to the actor Evan Austin.

She still couldn't believe it. Pauling vowed to keep an even demeanor with the actor but she was angry about the deceit and determined to find out why an actor from Brooklyn had played a part in sending her to Belize to investigate a missing boy.

Pauling parked the SUV and knocked on the door. It was a classic Brooklyn three-story house where each floor was its own flat. She was guessing Austin's would be on the first floor, and she was right. Older people tended to avoid stairs.

After ringing the doorbell and waiting, the door opened and Pauling came face-to-face with the actor who'd done such a good job of playing the attorney Randall Naughton.

"Hello, Mr. Austin, do you mind if I come in and have a word?"

The older man's face registered fear and for a moment she thought he was going to try to shut the door in her face.

"You are not in any danger," Pauling said. "I just want to ask you a few questions."

She stepped up to prevent the door closing and Austin must have realized the play was over.

He nodded and stepped back.

There was a hallway leading back toward a kitchen and off to the right, a small room that was probably once a parlor. There were two wing backed chairs and Austin gestured her to one.

"I'm sorry–" he began but Pauling cut him off.

"No need to apologize," she said. "You were doing what you do, right? Acting?"

"Yes, and I was told there was nothing illegal going on."

Pauling smiled. "Of course. And there wasn't. However, I'm wondering if you can tell me who hired you."

"I don't know," he said.

"What do you mean? Were you paid?"

"Yes, of course. But I was contacted via email and paid electronically. I never met my employer. But it was a very good fee."

"I see," Pauling said. She considered her options. "When I told you that you'd done nothing illegal, I wasn't being totally honest," she finally said. "As you know, my name is Lauren Pauling, I worked for the FBI for over twenty years and until recently ran one of the most successful private security firms in the world."

Now, the actor sat back, leaning away from Pauling. The fear was on his face again.

"Your employer, via you, asked me to investigate the disappearance of a boy, as you know," Pauling continued. "Well, the boy is dead. And there is the suspicion of foul play," she lied. "So unless you agree to help me now, at some point the authorities may come calling to find out more about you. Do you understand what I'm saying?"

"But I don't know anything!" Austin exclaimed. "It was all done anonymously. They sent me a script and promised me ten thousand dollars. They gave me a cell phone to use."

He hopped up out of the chair, ducked out of the room and came back. He handed a phone to her that was clearly a burner, designed to be used once and then thrown away.

"Did you receive any calls on it?"

"Only the call from you."

"Okay, I'm going to need a copy of your email correspondence, the account from which your payment was made. Everything. Otherwise, I'm going to contact the authorities in Belize and the FBI as well, telling them that you were possibly involved in a conspiracy to commit murder."

It was an exaggeration, but founded in truth.

And it scared the hell out of Evan Austin.

Within fifteen minutes, Pauling had all of the man's emails and bank receipts for the payment he'd earned deceiving her.

She left him then, with strict instructions not to reach back out to her employer. He was to say nothing to anyone, and she would do her best to keep his name out of anything that might develop.

Pauling got back into her SUV.

She was sure the email and bank payments would be hard to trace, but she also knew it wouldn't be impossible.

Pauling had the perfect man for the job. Still sitting outside the actor's home, she keyed in the relevant information, including emails, phone numbers, photos of the bank statements, and even the serial number of the burner phone and sent them from her phone to her former client. He was one of the best in the shadowy business of cybercrime.

Having done that, Pauling put the SUV in gear and started home.

She was hoping by the time she got there, some answers would have arrived.

Chapter 24

It was going to take Pauling twice as long to get into Manhattan as it did for her to get out.

She drove in stop-and-go traffic, thinking about Belize, Rubi and the poor boy who'd washed up on the beach, dead.

As much as she thought about possible scenarios, Pauling continued to come up with very little. It seemed like such an elaborate ruse; someone had to hire an actor to hire her, probably knowing she would have been suspicious of an anonymous email, and got her to investigate a disappearance.

They'd also done their research on her and knew that she had a history with Jack Reacher, which they dangled in front of her. Pauling was now more convinced than ever it was a complete fabrication designed to ensure her involvement.

But why?

What had they hoped she would learn in Belize?

A white panel van cut in front of her and Pauling had to slam on her brakes to avoid hitting the vehicle.

Where did they think they were going, exactly?

She put her blinker on to try to switch lanes when suddenly the rear doors of the panel van swung open and Pauling saw a man with a rifle pointing at her. She dropped to the floor as her windshield exploded. The sound of automatic gunfire was deafening and she heard bullets punching into the vehicle all around her.

Pauling threw herself over the passenger seat and landed in the middle of her vehicle as it crashed into the shoulder of the embankment.

Something hit her hard and low and she knew she'd been shot. Pauling fumbled for the door's latch release on the rear passenger door. It opened and she slid out of the vehicle, landing awkwardly on the pavement.

She snatched the small automatic she carried on her hip beneath her shirt. It was no match for the firepower she was facing. Pauling struggled to stand, but almost fell as her left leg and hip were completely numb.

A face appeared near the driver's door of her SUV and Pauling fired. The man spun and his gun fired harmlessly into the air. A shadow fell over her and she glanced up, knowing she'd made a mistake.

A second man was on top of her vehicle, looking down. But he was looking on the wrong side. Pauling brought her gun up just as he did. Pauling was faster and she fired first. The shot hit him just above his right ear and a tuft of hair lifted, followed by a geyser of blood and brain matter. His rifle barrel flamed and Pauling felt the blow in her right shoulder.

Her gun flew from her hand and she landed on her side.

She could just see around the back of the SUV. Tires squealed. An engine roared.

Pauling saw the panel van racing ahead, careening off cars stuck in the traffic jam. It had gone all the way onto the median and would soon be out of sight.

She looked down at the first man she'd shot. He had landed near her driver's side door. Her bullet had hit him in the neck and he'd bled profusely. His eyes were wide open and unblinking. He was dead.

Pauling heard sirens in the distance.

I wonder if I'll die before they can reach me, she thought. *This traffic really sucks.*

Chapter 25

Tallon arrived at the intensive care unit still in disbelief. He'd finished his security gig and been in the Mexico City airport about to fly back to the US when he'd gotten the phone call from Pauling's sister, who'd just been notified that a shooting had taken place. Pauling had been shot but she was alive.

The flight to New York was agony for Tallon and he raced to the hospital. He and Pauling's sister arrived at the same time. Tallon embraced Julia and together, they'd met with the ICU surgeon who explained the situation.

"She was shot twice and the damage was extensive," the doctor began. "However, the good news is no internal organs were damaged."

"Thank God," Julia said.

"She was shot in the right hip and in addition

to soft flesh, muscle and ligament damage, a piece of bone was shattered. We removed the fragments and repaired the bulk of the bone so she shouldn't suffer any permanent damage.

"Similarly, her second wound was to her right arm, just beneath the shoulder. Again, she was very lucky in that the joint remained intact. Obviously, the arm was broken and we knitted everything back together carefully. Blood loss wasn't too bad, and she's stable. In fact, she'll be moved out of ICU within the next twenty-four hours.

"Can we see her?" Tallon asked.

"Yes, she's coming out of anesthesia so she may be a little sleepy and unfocused. But you can talk to her – not too long, though as she needs her rest."

They thanked the surgeon and the surgical nurse escorted them back to Pauling's room.

She was flat on her back and Tallon thought she'd never looked more beautiful. Her startling green eyes recognized him and she smiled at her sister.

"Hey guys," she said. Her voice was even lower and huskier than normal.

"You had a gunfight and didn't invite me?" Tallon asked.

Pauling gave a tired smile and looked like she was about to drift off to sleep.

"Lauren, we talked to the surgeon," Julia said.

"You're going to be fine. I'm going to have all of your records sent to Steve, just so he can keep tabs." Tallon knew that Julia's husband, Steven, was a doctor in Portland, Oregon. A neurologist, he remembered.

"Okay," Pauling said.

Her eyes were half-dropping and Julia said, "We'll let you get some sleep."

"Wait," Pauling said. Her eyes had opened again and were focused on Tallon.

"Get my phone and look at the last message I sent," she said. "I need to find out—"

Her voice trailed off and her eyes closed. This time, she was asleep.

"Okay," Tallon said.

He and Julia left. Julia went to call her husband and Tallon went and spoke with the nurse. Julia had already signed for the things the paramedics had brought from the scene. Now, Tallon found Pauling's phone and saw the messages regarding the Belize investigation. He forwarded them to his own phone and was about to put Pauling's phone back in the bin with her other belongings when Pauling's phone pinged as a new message arrived.

Tallon double-tapped the new email icon and read with interest the response. This, too, he forwarded to his own phone.

"Are you a member of Lauren Pauling's family?" a voice asked.

Tallon turned to see a tall black man holding up a detective's shield for him to see. NYPD homicide.

"No, just a friend," he said.

"I see. Well, we may have some questions for you later."

The man took down Tallon's information.

"Busy day," the black man said. "This shootout and then another murder just down the road."

"Oh yeah?" Tallon asked.

"Yeah, must be something in the air. An old guy, an actor I'd seen once or twice on Broadway, was gunned down just before this one. Evan Austin was his name. Too bad, he was good on stage."

The detective looked at Tallon for any signs of recognition.

Not seeing any, he shrugged his shoulders.

"Well, like I said, we may want to talk to you later."

Tallon watched him walk away and wondered, *what in the world have you gotten yourself into, Pauling?"*

Chapter 26

Rayce was convinced he had killed the boy at the school. He was an expert marksman and never missed. He knew his shots had been spot on, the boy had fallen backward as the rounds tore into his chest.

Rayce had driven away convinced the boy was dead and he'd fulfilled his contract.

Until he searched for news of the shooting online.

He'd made it off of Cape Cod, sped down to New York and checked into a luxury hotel in Manhattan. Now, he had showered and was wrapped in a plush bathrobe with a bottle of champagne on ice. He held his champagne glass in one hand and with the other, he clicked on the news article regarding the school shooting in Massachusetts.

No deaths.

Only one injured.

Rayce leaned forward. All expression of satisfaction left his face. *No deaths?* How?

He skimmed the article for more information.

When he got to the section that described the boy's backpack, he shook his head in disbelief. It seemed that school shootings had gotten so out of hand in America that some intrepid entrepreneur had invented a backpack fitted with bulletproof Kevlar. The same kind of material used in bulletproof vests by police and SWAT teams.

It seemed the boy had one and now, Rayce remembered the boy holding the backpack in front of his body, digging for something at the bottom. The bullets Rayce had fired, which he had assumed would easily tear through a flimsy backpack, had simply knocked the boy down.

"Shit," Rayce muttered. What were the odds?

He sipped the champagne and knew that his employer would be calling any minute. She had no idea that in his profession, sometimes things went haywire. Expect the unexpected.

Well, there was one thing he could be sure of.

His boss was going to be very upset and she was not the kind of woman anyone would want to anger.

Chapter 27

Tallon spent two more hours by Pauling's bedside and then left her care to Julia and the nurses. He also arranged for extra security outside Pauling's room. Men he knew and could trust.

Tallon had no idea if the people who'd tried to kill Pauling would try again, but it was better to be safe.

He was anxious to get to work as he was intrigued by what he'd read on Pauling's phone.

Tallon took an Uber back to Pauling's condo and let himself in with the security code she'd given him.

He'd spent enough time in the home to be comfortable and he knew his way around. The first thing he did was to unpack the basics in terms of toiletries and a few items of clothes, and then he got right to work.

Tallon went into Pauling' home office and fired up her computer. He logged onto his own email server and reread the messages he'd forwarded to himself from Pauling's phone.

They were intriguing.

The email she'd gotten from the actor and sent to her online investigator had been traced.

There were two surprises: the first being that the sender had gone to great lengths to disguise the origination point of the message. Pauling's investigator had tracked the address across half the globe. Which meant that it was very important to someone to remain anonymous.

The second was the investigator's best guess at where the email had come from: Omaha, Nebraska.

Specifically, a suburban neighborhood.

Tallon had been expecting the location to be New York or Belize. But Omaha?

Still, he knew that Pauling hired only the best of the best so he wasn't going to doubt the conclusion.

Which meant he was going to have to go to Omaha.

Not yet, though. He still needed to figure out the big picture of what was going on. Luckily, Pauling had left all of the paperwork on the Belize case on her desk, including the initial assessment provided to her by Randall Naughton, the man

Tallon now knew was a dead actor named Evan Austin.

Tallon read the briefing material and also the report Pauling had compiled on her research in Belize, which she'd included with her final bill to the pretend attorney.

He read with great interest the Jack Reacher angle and agreed with Pauling's assessment that it was most likely not true.

Still, Pauling had conducted her investigation in Belize without knowing that she'd been set up.

The key, in Tallon's mind, was still on Ambergris Caye.

With Rubi.

Chapter 28

The woman in the penthouse apartment with views of Central Park was furious. Rayce had failed her. And now, after being tipped off to the presence of a private investigator looking into things with the help of all things, an actor, she'd been left with yet another disappointment. Her team had succeeded in killing the actor in Brooklyn but had failed to neutralize the woman who'd been poking around in Belize.

It was so hard to find good help these days, she thought.

She paced and finally decided that it wasn't her problem to solve.

It was Rayce's. She had already paid him a small fortune and he hadn't come through for her. Not even close.

He would have to solve everything; the last kid

he hadn't killed, this Lauren Pauling situation, and any other problems that came up. As in, she still wasn't sure who'd gotten this private investigator involved.

She was going to give Rayce one chance to make it right.

And if he failed, well, she would simply have to eliminate him.

A little sooner than she'd originally planned.

Chapter 29

Tallon wanted to explain to Pauling what he was doing, but she was sound asleep when he returned to the hospital. Julia was still by her side.

He decided to take a chance and he told Julia some of what was going on, keeping out anything that could potentially put her at risk. Tallon asked her to explain to Pauling where he'd gone. Julia understood both Tallon's line of work and her sister's, so she didn't ask too many prying questions.

She also understood that Tallon's goal was to ultimately help protect Pauling by figuring out what this boy's death in Belize was really all about.

From the hospital, Tallon went to the airport and took the same flight to Belize Pauling had. Unlike the slower sea ferry, however, he took a flight on a small plane from Belize City directly to

Ambergris Caye where he rented a car and drove straight to Rubi's coffee shop.

He'd made no arrangements for a place to stay.

Tallon was here for one thing only; the missing piece of the puzzle that he felt would bring clarity to the assassination attempt made on Pauling.

The building was neat, very tropical with its whitewashed walls, orange trim and green shutters. Very colorful and welcoming.

Tallon parked and went inside.

The interior was divided into two spaces. One was a more retail kind of space with a coffee counter, stools, tables and chairs. The other half had all the markings of a bigger, more commercial coffee enterprise. There were stacked boxes of coffee that looked like they were ready for transport and behind them, several large stainless steel kettles.

A scrawny man sitting at the coffee counter picked up his cup of coffee and left without saying a word.

There was no one else in the room.

Tallon went to the counter. He leaned across and peered into the rear of the building.

A woman was in the back, cleaning a large cylinder. The whole place smelled delicious to Tallon.

"Can I help you?" the woman asked as she approached.

Tallon was surprised at how beautiful she was, then again, why would Pauling put that in her notes? She was small, with long black hair tied into a ponytail and skin that was smooth as glass. Her almond-shaped eyes were friendly but cautious.

"Are you Rubi?" he asked. She wiped her hands on her dark green apron.

"Yes."

"First of all, I'm sorry about your son."

She narrowed her eyes at him but didn't say anything.

"I work with Lauren Pauling – the woman who was here a few days ago?"

Rubi started shaking her head. "I told her–"

"You told her the father of your son died a long time ago. That wasn't true, was it?"

Tallon was guessing, but it was the most likely scenario. Pauling hadn't challenged the woman because it hadn't been the time or the place. And she hadn't been operating with the same sense of urgency that he now was.

"If you want coffee, order some. If not, get out," Rubi said.

She glanced over his shoulders as the front door of the shop opened.

Tallon saw Rubi's eyes widen in alarm and she glanced at Tallon, as if to send him a warning.

He turned and saw a huge man wearing a khaki uniform with a black cap on his head. There was a badge affixed to its peak.

"You must be Deputy Jalisco," Tallon said with a smile.

"And who are you?"

"Just a friend of Rubi's."

Tallon glanced over Jalisco's mass and saw the little man who'd raced out of the coffee shop. A spy, no doubt. Sent to watch Rubi.

"Come with me, *friend*," Jalisco said.

Tallon glanced back at Rubi. "I'll be right back."

He walked past Jalisco, down the steps, and stood with his back to Rubi's shop. A San Pedro Land Rover was parked a few feet away. Tallon could see the shape of at least one person inside.

"You need to leave her alone," Jalisco said as he walked down the steps. The wooden planks groaned in protest.

"Why?"

"Because she is in mourning."

"And you're here to protect her?"

"Of course."

"Well, I'm here to help her. So you should be welcoming me to your cute little town, not trying to scare me off."

"You can help her by leaving her alone," Jalisco said. The night air was warm and Jalisco was sweating. "I know what is best for her. Not you."

"No," Tallon said.

Jalisco cocked his massive head toward Tallon. "Did you say no?"

"What I talk about with her is none of your business, Chubby," Tallon said.

Two of the doors to the Land Rover opened. A woman got out of one side. A man emerged from the other. He was short and muscular and he was grinning. He was also missing two teeth.

Unlike him, the woman was not smiling. In fact, she looked unhappy.

"Arrest him," Jalisco said.

The short man didn't hesitate. He charged Tallon. Apparently, he liked to wrestle because he was clearly going for a tackle of some sort, probably hoping to get Tallon on the ground and then Jalisco could sit on him.

It was clear to Tallon that the small policeman was not expecting resistance. Maybe the guy had played American football at some point and had used a tackling dummy. An inert object was easy to tackle.

Tallon was not going to remain inert.

He simply stepped forward and brought his right knee up in a savage half-kick that caught the charging man on the bridge of the nose. His head snapped back as Tallon's knee pushed its way against the cartilage, crushing it, and then fully contacting the man's forehead. Tallon felt the solid impact all the way to his bones.

The sound was nothing more than a dull thump, but the short policeman dropped to the ground.

Jalisco had seen enough. He stepped in with a leather sap and swung at Tallon's head. It must have been lead-weighted because it was a slow, sweeping maneuver that gave Tallon plenty of time to duck and deliver a straight right to the big man's belly.

The sap flew from Jalisco's hand and he leaned forward, a huge exhalation of breath leaving his mouth.

His face was contorted and Tallon simply pivoted and threw a short left hook that caught Jalisco flush on the jaw. This sounded different than the knee to the little man's head. This was all flesh and bone meeting more flesh and bone. The sound was vicious and seemed to echo in the night air.

Jalisco joined his subordinate on the ground and in a similar state of unconsciousness.

Tallon glanced over at the remaining cop, the woman, who still hadn't moved. She stood next to the Land Rover, looking down at her colleagues with not an ounce of sympathy. In fact, Tallon thought she might have been smiling.

"Leave and don't come back," he told her.

She turned on her heel and walked away into the night.

Tallon made sure neither man was carrying a gun and then he went back inside the coffee shop.

Rubi was standing by the front door, looking through one of the windows. She'd seen everything.

"Now," Tallon said, "it's time for you to tell me the truth."

Chapter 30

The dark sea was to their left. All traces of sunlight gone, it lay upon the murky horizon in striations of purple, black and dark blue.

"Where are you taking me?" Rubi asked.

"Far enough away so you can claim I kidnapped you and forced you to give me the information I need," Tallon said. "The truth in other words – that those clowns back there were paid to protect, am I right?"

The car's instrument panel gave off enough light that Tallon saw the nearly imperceptible nod of her head.

"They said they would kill me if I said anything to you or the woman who was here before."

"Why?"

"Someone paid them, of course," Rubi answered. "There would be no other reason."

Tallon drove on in silence.

"I don't know what I'm afraid of," she said at last. "They killed my son." She started sobbing. "But my mother lives with me. They said they would kill her if I said anything."

Tallon waited and then said, "It's about the boy's father, isn't it?"

Rubi cried again and when she finally spoke, it was tinged with anger. "Yes."

"He's not dead, is he?"

"Unfortunately, no. If he was here now, he would be dead because I would kill him with my bare hands."

Tallon said nothing as a golf cart passed them going in the opposite direction.

"Who is he?"

Rubi gave a ragged sigh.

"Remember, tell them I was going to kill you if you didn't tell me," Tallon told her.

Finally Rubi spoke. "He's an American. His name is David Silver."

Tallon looked at her. "David Silver as in Silver Apps?"

Rubi snorted.

Tallon had heard of the man. He'd developed some of the first apps for mobile phones and made hundreds of millions of dollars. Tallon vaguely remembered reading that he'd sold his company and moved somewhere in the Caribbean.

"I was working in a coffee shop as a waitress when he met me," Rubi explained. "Promised me all kinds of things. He was handsome, though. A big guy, like you. Once I was pregnant, he told me to get an abortion. I left, instead. Eventually, he did, too. I never heard from him again."

"I'm sorry, Rubi," Tallon said.

"Don't be. I'm glad I never talked to him or received any money from him. I knew I had to take care of myself. I just—"

Tallon saw lights ahead and knew he was at the set of docks he'd been aiming for. He'd arranged to have a boat standing by just in case he needed to get off the island and back to the mainland in a hurry.

"I just never knew that I wouldn't be able to escape him," Ruby said.

"You think your son was killed, don't you?" Tallon asked.

"Yes, of course."

"And that it has something to do with David Silver?"

"Yes, someone with money. If not David, then maybe someone who wanted to hurt him. Who else could afford to pay off the entire San Pedro police force? No one around here, that's for sure. And now my Peter is dead."

Rubi burst into tears again and Tallon put his arm around her shoulders. She leaned against him.

He pulled out all of the cash he'd brought with him and gave it to her. She didn't look at the amount.

"I'm going to find out who did this," he told her.

"And then what?" she asked, her voice sounding faint.

"I'm going to make them pay for what they've done."

She slid across the front seat and behind the wheel of the rental car.

"Be careful," she said and drove away.

Chapter 31

It was suicide.

If Rayce tried to go back to Cape Cod and kill the kid, he'd never make it. They'd know by now it wasn't a school shooting. One witness for sure saw him try to shoot the little bastard. The cops would find the slugs in the kid's fricking Kevlar backpack – who would ever think such a thing even existed!

Rayce was so angry. He should've gone for a head shot.

Next time, he thought.

For now, he was told he needed to go to Omaha and put down the last one. He'd agreed to do it, but at the moment he was having second thoughts. He knew that the woman he was working for didn't tolerate mistakes. It would be so easy for her to set him up. Call the cops ahead of time, have them waiting for him in Omaha.

Get him on Murder One and he'd rot in prison for the rest of his life.

No thank you.

No, he wasn't rushing to Nebraska anytime soon.

Plus, he was already in New York. She told him about the private detective that had killed two of her men during an ambush on the highway. It seemed he wasn't the only one who'd let her down.

Rayce wondered if she was going to try to tie up that loose end on her own. The PI would no doubt be under heavy protection wherever she was.

He felt cornered. Damned if he did, damned if he didn't.

Even twenty-five floors up, he could hear the sound of New York traffic. Cars honking. Even people yelling occasionally. Nothing like an angry city to drive a person to contemplate strategies for survival.

What he knew was that Cape Cod was a dead end for him. Omaha was risky, too. So was trying to finish off the private detective in the hospital.

There was one other option he had considered.

It too was dangerous.

But it would be the least expected. It wouldn't earn him any more money, but it would guarantee the funds he'd already been paid. Long-term it might be the best option.

He walked to the closet and looked at the clothes he had hanging there. Only one suit but it was his best one.

That was good, he thought, *because I'm headed uptown*.

Chapter 32

Tallon was relieved to see there was a direct flight from Belize to Miami. He timed it perfectly and when the ground fell away and his window was filled with reflection of the Caribbean sea below, he felt even better.

He wasn't sure how fast Deputy Jalisco could have alerted authorities in Belize City, or if he'd even wanted to. Perhaps the bribes had applied to only the San Pedro Police. If Jalisco had been able to organize a welcoming party for Tallon, it was too late now.

In any event, Tallon was glad when the plane lifted off.

Miami soon came into view and he marveled at the difference between the US and places like Belize. The city's high rises and packed web of freeways spoke of the congested population. As sleepy as Belize City had been, Miami in contrast was wide awake twenty-four hours a day.

The plane landed and Tallon soon departed the airport in a rented SUV, white of course, and set out to find David Silver.

He knew it wouldn't be easy.

That's why he had paid for Internet usage aboard the plane and sent out messages to his own contacts as well as the man Pauling had worked with. Pauling's guy came through first.

It was an address in Fort Lauderdale, home of the legendary college spring break escapades and a small city in its own right.

Tallon made it to the suburb of Miami in a little over forty-five minutes and used his phone's navigation app to direct him to the supposed home address of Silver.

It was a high-rise tower of condominiums facing the ocean. The building was at least fifty stories high, clad in a white exterior with a façade that was shaved off at an angle so every unit had a view of the water. That way, the developers could ask more money for each individual condo.

He had his doubts on the potential for success-fully finding his quarry. A guy like Silver probably had multiple homes in several countries not to mention a yacht or two. Tallon was pleased that Pauling's investigator had determined that Silver's automobiles were all registered to this address,

which meant it was most likely his primary resi-
dence. Plus, there had been online speculation of
Silver's flamboyant Miami lifestyle.

Tallon parked the SUV in a visitor's parking
space and then went inside the building where he
found a security guard parked at a front desk.
Being such a highly prestigious address, one
simply wasn't allowed to hop in an elevator
and go.

"I'm here to see David Silver," Tallon told the
security guard. He had close-cropped gray hair
and a scar along his neck. An ex-cop, Tallon
figured.

"Your name"

"Michael Tallon."

The guard run a stubby finger along the
computer screen in front of him.

"I don't see your name on the guest list."

"He's not expecting me, but he'll be very
happy to see me. Tell him Rubi Gemmot sent me,
from Belize."

"Have a seat," the guard said gesturing with a
tilt of his head toward a white leather couch
across the room.

Tallon followed his directions and waited. He
watched the guard pick up a phone and talk for a
moment, look at Tallon a couple of times and
then he finally hung up the phone.

"Okay, Mr. Tallon. Mr. Silver will see you."

The guard held out a temporary pass with a key card.

"Use this to unlock the elevator. Mr. Silver is unit 700 on the 7th floor."

The guard smirked a little bit and Tallon wondered why. He went into the elevator, held the card against a sensor and pressed the 7 button. It whisked him up silently and when the doors opened, he saw that there were two doors on each side of the hall. One read 700, the other 701. The hallway was plush white carpet. The walls were done in a mirrored wallpaper of sorts. The effect was strange and hypnotic.

Tallon went to 700 and rang the bell.

A woman answered.

She was Asian, dressed in a bikini, with a line of white powder across the top of her lip.

"Lookeee here," she slurred.

From behind her, a man stepped out. He was tall, easily 6'5" with broad shoulders and a narrow waist. Muscles bulged and popped in his shoulders and arms. He was dressed in a pair of jockey shorts and nothing else. A strange wiry tattoo ran the length of his torso. His spiky hair was bleached blond and he had a martini glass in one hand and a gun in the other.

He studied Tallon with a wild intensity, like a man about to leap into a firefight.

"How's that bitch Rubi?" he asked.

Chapter 33

"She believes her son was killed. Or should I say, your son?" Tallon answered. David Silver looked nothing like the man Tallon had remembered from news stories. In those, he'd always been impeccably dressed in expensive suits, surrounded by corporate backdrops that screamed success on Wall Street.

The man in front of him looked like some kind of wild animal. Hair in disarray, his eyes wide due no doubt to some sort of chemical ingestion. The gun didn't help lend any normalcy to the visual.

The Asian girl had suddenly disappeared. Loud rock music was blaring and Silver crossed the room, punched a button and silence filled the space.

"What did you say?" he asked Tallon.

"Peter. Rubi's son. He died. The authorities say he drowned. Rubi thinks otherwise."

"He wasn't mine," Silver answered. "Rubi thought so. Everyone did. But he wasn't."

Silver chugged whatever liquid was in his martini glass and set it on a marble-topped table. He placed the gun down, too.

"Who the hell are you, anyway?" he finally asked.

"A friend of a friend who went to investigate the boy's disappearance. She asked me to help and I'm here trying to find out who would have wanted to hurt the boy."

"How the hell would I know? Hey, you want something to drink? Want some blow?"

Tallon shook his head as Silver leaned his head down to the table and snorted a line of cocaine. As the drugs hit his system he did a weird little dance move.

"Maybe someone was trying to blackmail you," Tallon suggested. "Grab your boy and make you pay for his safe release."

"Not my goddamn kid, I said," Silver barked at him. His eyes narrowed and Tallon thought the man might try to charge him.

But then he relented with a big grin. "Besides, don't you read the news? I'm broke and destined for the slammer. By the time the courts get done with me there won't be shit left. That's why I threw a party about two years ago and it's still going on."

Tallon looked around the space. He vaguely remembered something about lawsuits over the copyrights to some of Silver's apps.

"You live pretty well for someone who's bankrupt," Tallon pointed out.

"Yeah, but it's almost all gone." The Asian girl in the bikini walked past him and he slapped her on the ass. "When it's gone, she'll be gone, too," Silver said and laughed hysterically. Then his face became gravely serious. "I know who probably took that boy."

Tallon wasn't sure he'd heard right.

"You do?"

"Yeah, come here." Silver waved Tallon forward and he followed his host down a hallway to a screening room with an enormous projection television and theater-style seats.

Silver went to a cupboard to the right of the screen and opened it.

It was empty.

"Know what I had in there?"

"More guns?"

"No, smart ass. Movies. Not just any movies, though. They all starred me – you follow?"

"Yeah, I think I get it," Tallon said. Silver seemed like the kind of guy who would make videos of himself having sex with various women. He seemed to fit the bill in terms of being an egomaniac.

"They're gone! Someone stole them!" Silver laughed. "Imagine that! I still can't believe they're not plastered all over YouTube – which makes me wonder – what are they doing with them?"

"Has anyone tried to blackmail you over them?"

"Of course not – I would have told you that. The cops, too."

Tallon saw the logic. "So you think if they're not posting them to the Internet and they're not blackmailing you over them, they must be using them for something else."

"Yeah, but what?"

Tallon thought about Rubi. About how she'd said no one locally would have the kind of money required to pay off the San Pedro Police. But what if they weren't paying them off? What if, instead, they were promising them a share of some bigger payday down the road?

A thought emerged from the possible scenarios and Tallon's mind turned it over several different ways. Something felt right about it to him.

"Do you have kids?"

"Hell no, I got the snip-snip years ago so I can

bang these hotties without a condom," Silver said, making a thrusting motion with his hips. "It's also why I don't have kids and how I know that boy in Belize ain't mine."

Tallon didn't believe a word of what Silver was saying, but he decided to set that issue aside.

"If you don't lose everything, but you die, who gets your fortune?"

"Ha! My crazy bitch ex-wife, that's who. Gloria. Which is why I'm spending every last penny I have. Gloria can kiss my ass if she thinks she's getting a penny out of me."

"These movies of yours – how many were there?"

"Quite a few."

"Okay, let me clarify. How many different women?"

Silver cocked his head. "Just a few."

"Was Rubi in one of them?"

Silver had a cagey look on his face and Tallon instantly knew that Rubi, and probably some of the other women in the videos, hadn't known they were being filmed.

"Maybe."

"Did any of the women claim you fathered a child?"

"Well, Rubi did. I told her she was nuts. Two other women did, too."

"In Belize?"

Silver shook his head.

"No. One was up near Boston. The other was in Omaha."

Chapter 34

Rayce had visited Gloria Silver's luxury apartment overlooking Central Park once before.

It was when she'd first laid out the scope of her plan. Three bastard children of David Silver's who could challenge her right to his estate. Kill them all, and then finally, kill David himself.

Now, that plan hadn't worked out. He'd gotten the kid in Belize, but the one in Cape Cod with his Kevlar backpack had changed everything.

Rayce had decided to skip going back to Massachusetts, and wasn't about to go after the last target in Omaha.

He had to stop Gloria, and stop her now.

With a nod to the doorman he rode the elevator to the penthouse and knocked on the door.

Gloria herself answered as he had texted her

to let her know he needed to speak with her. She hadn't been happy about it, but he'd left her no choice.

"Do you want a drink? It's five o'clock somewhere," Gloria said. She had a glass of whiskey in her hand.

"Sure."

He once again marveled at the size of the space. It was huge – with parquet floors, coffered ceilings and exquisite furnishings. It was the kind of apartment you saw only in magazines. The best features were the windows; huge expanses of glass with breathtaking views of Central Park. In the middle were French doors that led to a balcony enclosed with black wrought iron.

It must have cost a fortune just to keep this place going, Rayce thought. Hence, Gloria's plan.

She brought him a glass of whiskey.

"What's the problem?" she asked. "Other than your screw up in Boston?"

"No problem. I just had a thought I wanted to talk to you about."

"You had a thought? Get out," she chided.

"Listen," Rayce said, ignoring her jab. "It's just I was wondering what would happen if the courts still convict your ex-husband after he's dead? You know, after we kill him?"

Gloria Silver was a beautiful woman, even when she was irritated. Rayce found himself wanting to kiss her elegant lips. Her long black hair, elegant jawline all spoke of wealth and privilege.

"They won't," she said, her voice even. "With him dead, the cases will all be dismissed. Do you really believe I didn't think that through?"

Her pale blue eyes, shark's eyes, bore into him.

"I want to show you something," she said.

Rayce followed her, his eyes drawn to her hips. He was going to kill her, for sure. But maybe he would have some fun with her first. He'd never had a woman like her before. He drank half of the whiskey in his glass, savored its smoky bite.

Gloria opened the French doors to the balcony and leaned against the waist-high black railing.

"This used to be David's," she said, turning and gesturing toward the apartment behind them. "He didn't want to give it to me, but I forced him to." She patted the railing next to her. "Come. You have to see it from this perspective."

Rayce crossed the patio and stood next to her. The penthouse apartment was spectacular. In his mind, he tried to calculate how much it was worth. Tens of millions of dollars certainly. He drank the rest of his whiskey.

Gloria stepped away from the railing and turned, facing Rayce. She put her hands on his shoulders and smiled at him. Their faces were only inches apart.

Rayce felt something stir deep within him. Desire. His stomach twisted and then twisted again. Sweat broke out along his forehead. No woman had ever made him feel like this. The sweat began to drip and his breath shortened. His throat tightened. His stomach twisted again, this time in pain. Stabbing pains pierced his abdomen.

He looked at the whiskey glass. It turned into three glasses all at once. They floated, out of focus beyond his reach.

"You," he started to say.

"Yes."

Gloria grabbed the front of his shirt and began to push his upper body over the railing.

Rayce's hands shot up and grabbed Gloria by the throat.

He couldn't breathe. His muscles spasmed but his hands held on. He felt himself going backward but he couldn't stop. Gloria stopped pushing and put her hands on his arms trying to break his grip.

But he was falling and she was on top of him.

They both went over the railing as Rayce's eyes rolled into the back of his head, the poison causing his veins to rupture and by the time they'd both fallen from the 70th floor, he was already dead, seconds before they both hit the ground.

Epilogue

Pauling unbuckled her seat belt as Tallon pulled the car to the curb. Her shoulder was still stiff and her hip was sore, but she was able to move without much pain.

It had been weeks since the shooting and although no arrests had been made, the detectives working her case had come to see her upon news of Gloria Silver's death.

A search of the woman's home had revealed messages involving Pauling as well as the actor Evan Austin.

The man who had died along with Gloria Silver, Rayce Baskins, was thought not to be involved in her shooting but he had been implicated in the attempted killing of a boy in Cape Cod. Also, a new autopsy had been ordered on the boy in Belize and the classification had been changed from drowning to murder. Rayce Baskins was also implicated in that killing.

Now, Tallon joined Pauling and they looked at the house. It was a turn-of-the-century bungalow, impeccably maintained and looking as definitively American as the rest of the homes in this historic neighborhood in Omaha.

For Pauling, it was the last piece of the puzzle.

She wasn't sure what she was going to find.

"Are you ready?" Pauling asked Tallon.

He nodded and she knew he was armed. A shoulder holster with a 9mm at the ready. Tallon walked up to the front door and rang the bell. Pauling stood at his shoulder, slightly behind him.

The door opened and a woman looked out at them. She was tall and athletic with short blonde hair. Pauling guessed she was in her late thirties or early forties. Very pretty.

"Yes?" the woman said.

"Is Joe home?" Pauling's cyber investigator had eventually tracked down the owner of the email account that had been used to hire Evan Austin and, in turn, Pauling.

The woman's face registered curiosity. No fear.

"Yes. May I ask why you want to see him?"

"He's a friend, that's all. My name is Lauren Pauling and this is Michael Tallon."

"Wait here," she said. She shut the door and Pauling knew she'd locked it, too.

"Can't blame her for being cautious," Tallon said.

They heard footsteps and then the door opened. This time, it was a young man. Very tall. With broad shoulders, sandy brown hair and blue eyes.

He gave a shy smile.

"Hi," he said. "I figured you might stop by."

Tallon and Pauling joined the young man in the living room. The mother hovered nearby. Pauling wasn't sure how much the woman knew.

"Do you know what happened to the actor you hired?" Pauling began.

"Yes," Joe said. The smile left his face. "I never meant for him to get hurt."

"I know," Pauling answered. "It wasn't your fault."

The young man didn't respond.

His mother shifted her stance and he glanced over at her. "Can you give us a minute, Mom?" he asked.

She left then and Pauling heard her start to unload the dishwasher in the kitchen.

"How did you find out what was happening in Belize?" Tallon asked.

Joe looked up at them, his blue eyes blazing. "My Mom told me about *him*. He stopped by once when I was little."

Pauling heard dishes rattle in the kitchen and she knew the boy was talking about David Silver.

"I was always really good with computers and even though my Mom said he wasn't my Dad, I started doing some research," Joe said. "I found out there might be a couple others like me. So I started keeping tabs on them. When I learned about Rubi's son, I needed someone to investigate. So I borrowed some of his money and used it to fund my own research, including the thief I hired to grab his movie collection and destroy it."

"But how–" Tallon started to ask. Pauling put her hand on his arm and he stopped his question.

"I understand," she said to Joe. She meant she understood more than the fact that the boy had somehow stolen some of David Silver's money, but also why he'd chosen her.

Joe looked at her, puzzled. She glanced toward the kitchen and then back at the boy. Recognition lit up his eyes and then the shy smile appeared again.

"Your Mom's name is Lisa?" Pauling asked.

The noises in the kitchen stopped. The woman appeared again in the doorway. "Okay, Joe, time to finish your studies. You've got an exam tomorrow."

The young man stood and Pauling was again struck by his physical presence. It reminded her of someone she once knew very well.

They said their goodbyes and back in the car Tallon started the engine.

He turned and looked at Pauling.

"I don't think I totally understand."

Pauling smiled.

"His mother's name is Lisa. Last name Harper."

"Joe Harper. Yeah, we knew that."

"There was a Lisa Harper in the FBI who was involved in a case with Jack Reacher. I remember reading about the case after I'd already left the Bureau."

A boy with a dog on a leash passed them on the sidewalk. The boy was trying to get the dog to walk next to him, but the smells around the trees were too interesting and the dog kept pulling the boy sideways.

"I still don't understand," Tallon said.

"It's how Joe found me. He must've known about his mother's relationship with Reacher and since the kid is obviously good with computers and online research, he somehow found out about me and my history with Reacher. It's why he dropped the clue about Reacher to get me to go to Belize."

"So do you think Joe is Reacher's son or Silver's?"

Pauling thought about the answer. "I don't

know and I don't care to. It's none of my business."

Tallon took that as his cue. He put the car in gear and drove down the street.

Pauling watched the houses go by. They all had picket fences, neat porches and big oak trees shading lush green lawns.

Not a bad place to grow up, she thought. A bright young man like Joe Harper, well, he could grow up to be anything and anyone he wanted to be.

Anyone at all.

NEW! The JACK REACHER
Cases

A MAN BORN
FOR BATTLE

by

Dan Ames

AUTHORDANAMES.COM

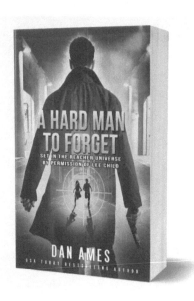

Book One in The JACK REACHER Cases

AUTHORDANAMES.COM

A Fast-Paced Action-Packed
Thriller Series

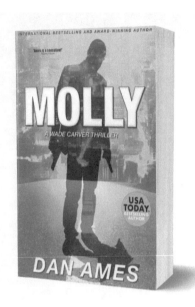

AUTHORDANAMES.COM

Also by Dan Ames

THE JACK REACHER CASES

The JACK REACHER Cases #1 (A Hard Man To Forget)

The JACK REACHER Cases #2 (The Right Man For Revenge)

The JACK REACHER Cases #3 (A Man Made For Killing)

The JACK REACHER Cases #4 (The Last Man To Murder)

The JACK REACHER Cases #5 (The Man With No Mercy)

The JACK REACHER Cases #6 (A Man Out For Blood)

The JACK REACHER Cases #7 (A Man Beyond The Law)

The JACK REACHER Cases #8 (The Man Who Walks Away)

The JACK REACHER Cases (The Man Who Strikes Fear)

The JACK REACHER Cases (The Man Who Stands Tall)

The JACK REACHER Cases (The Man Who Works Alone)

JACK REACHER'S SPECIAL INVESTIGATORS

BOOK ONE: DEAD MEN WALKING

BOOK TWO: GAME OVER

BOOK THREE: LIGHTS OUT

BOOK FOUR: NEVER FORGIVE, NEVER FORGET

BOOK FIVE: HIT THEM FAST, HIT THEM HARD

BOOK SIX: FINISH THE FIGHT

JACK REACHER'S SPECIAL INVESTIGATORS

BOOK ONE: DEAD MEN WALKING

BOOK TWO: GAME OVER

BOOK THREE: LIGHTS OUT

BOOK FOUR: NEVER FORGIVE, NEVER
FORGET

BOOK FIVE: HIT THEM FAST, HIT
THEM HARD

BOOK SIX: FINISH THE FIGHT

THE JOHN ROCKNE MYSTERIES

THE WADE CARVER THRILLERS

THE WALLACE MACK THRILLERS

THE MARY COOPER MYSTERIES

DEATH BY SARCASM (Mary Cooper Mystery #1)

MURDER WITH SARCASTIC INTENT (Mary Cooper Mystery #2)

GROSS SARCASTIC HOMICIDE (Mary Cooper Mystery #3)

THE CIRCUIT RIDER (WESTERNS)

THE RAY MITCHELL THRILLERS

THE RECRUITER

KILLING THE RAT

HEAD SHOT

SHORT STORIES:

THE GARBAGE COLLECTOR

BULLET RIVER

SCHOOL GIRL

HANGING CURVE

SCALE OF JUSTICE

Free Books And More

**Would you like a FREE copy
of my story BULLET RIVER and the
chance
to win a free Kindle?**

**Then sign up for the DAN AMES BOOK
CLUB:**

AUTHORDANAMES.COM